GIRL

Surf Girls

Shey Kettle

to: Haily from: Jordan
happy b-day

illustrated by
Meredith Thomas

First published in 2005 by
MACMILLAN EDUCATION AUSTRALIA PTY LTD
627 Chapel Street, South Yarra 3141
Reprinted 2005

Visit our web site at www.macmillan.com.au

Associated companies and representatives throughout the world.

Copyright © Felice Arena, Phil Kettle and Shey Kettle 2005

All rights reserved.
Except under the conditions described in the *Copyright Act 1968* of Australia and subsequent amendments, no part of this publication may be reproduced, stored in a retrieval system, or transmitted in any form or by any means, electronic, mechanical, photocopying, recording or otherwise, without the prior written permission of the copyright owner.

National Library of Australia
Cataloguing-in-Publication data

Kettle, Shey.

   Surf girls.

   For primary school students.
   ISBN 0 7329 9882 4.
   ISBN 0 7329 9876 X (series).

   1. Surfing – Juvenile fiction. I. Title. (Series: Girlz rock!).

A823.4

Series created by Felice Arena and Phil Kettle
Project Management by Limelight Press Pty Ltd
Cover and text design by Lore Foye
Illustrations by Meredith Thomas

Printed in Australia by McPherson's Printing Group

GIRLZ ROCK!
Contents

CHAPTER 1
Let's Go!   1

CHAPTER 2
Sand Stepping   7

CHAPTER 3
Wave Riders   14

CHAPTER 4
The Surf-off   22

CHAPTER 5
Double Trouble   28

EXTRA STUFF

- Surfing Lingo   33
- Surfing Must-dos   34
- Surfing Instant Info   36
- Think Tank   38
- Hey Girls! (Author Letter)   40
- When We Were Kids   42
- What a Laugh!   43

Mai   Carly

CHAPTER 1

Let's Go!

Best friends Carly and Mai are excited. The summer school holidays have started and they are off to the beach. Mai's mum has promised the girls that as they've been good, they can stay in a caravan by the beach for a few days.

Carly "I can't wait till we get there."

Mai "Yeah, it'll be heaps of fun."

Carly "Especially now that our dorky brothers aren't coming. Boys just have no idea how to be good!"

Mai "Well, they were until we tricked them into showing us how fast they could swing on the clothes line. Pity Mum caught them."

Carly "Yeah, real pity! So now it'll just be us girls at the beach."

Mai "How much fun is this gonna be!"

Carly "I know, and staying in a caravan, too."

Mai "Cool as."

Carly and Mai help to pack the car and put their boogie boards in the back. Then they all head off for the coast. The girls sit in the back seat talking about what they will do when they get to the beach.

Carly "I reckon I could be the best surfer in the world."

Mai "You mean you could be the third best surfer in the world, if you're lucky!"

Carly "What d'you mean? Who could be better than me?"

Mai "Well, for a start, there's Layne Beachley, she's been a world champion. And, the other one ... um ... is well ... let me think ... ah that's right, *me*!"

Carly "In your dreams! There's no way that you're better than me."

Mai "Well, I think we might just have to have a contest. A surf-off, to see who the real surf girl champion is!"

CHAPTER 2

Sand Stepping

In no time at all, the family car pulls up at the caravan park. Mai and Carly jump out and start unpacking. Then they head towards the beach.

Mai "Look at the size of the waves."

Carly "They're humungous. The biggest waves I've ever seen."

Mai "How good would you have to be to surf these waves!"

Carly "I told you in the car—as good as me."

Mai "Yeah, right."

Carly "Yeow! This path is hot! Beat ya down to the sand dunes."

Mai "You're on!"

The girls race down a sand dune that leads down to the beach. Mai narrowly beats Carly. They sit down and wait for Mai's mother to arrive so that they can hit the surf.

Mai "Beat ya!"

Carly "Maybe this time, but wait till we get out to those waves—I'll show you!"

Mai "I'd love to be a dolphin."

Carly "I'd rather be a shark."

Mai "Dolphins are the best surfers in the world."

Carly "Sharks are too. They're cool!"

Mai "Why? Because they've been around since the dinosaurs, have a million teeth and can smell blood from miles away?"

Carly "No, because they rule the sea. Everyone gets outta *their* way."

Mai "At Ocean World last year, I got to hold the hoop while a dolphin jumped through. Bet you've never seen sharks do that."

Carly "No, but I've seen them make heaps of swimmers leave the beach in less than 30 seconds."

Mai "Sharks could never match dolphins—just like you won't be able to match me when we surf."

Mai's mother comes walking down the path to where the girls are waiting. After putting the umbrella in the sand, she tells Carly and Mai that they can go in the water, but they must swim between the flags.

CHAPTER 3

Wave Riders

The girls put on their wetsuits, then pick up their boards as they run to the water. They both yell "Here we come!" at the same time as they splash into the surf.

Carly "This is so cool."

Mai "I'm gonna invent my own boogie board trick, one that no-one has ever seen before."
Carly "I'd like to see that."

The voice of the lifeguard roars out from the loudspeakers attached to lifeguard tower: "Can you stay between the flags please?"

Carly "This is so awesome. I just love boogie boarding."

Mai "So do I. How cool is this!"

Carly and Mai don't hear the lifeguard and keep catching waves.

Mai "Girls are so smart."

Carly "Why do you say that?"

Mai "Because we can do three things at the same time—surf, talk and think. Boys could never do that."

Carly "Yeah, but I've seen my brother do two things at the same time."

Mai "Like what?"

Carly "Run and pick his zits!"

Both girls laugh. Mai looks up and sees her mother standing on the water's edge. She's waving a towel and holding up the food basket. The girls race back into shore.

Carly "I'm starving. And so are these seagulls. There's a million of them."

Mai "Seagulls must have some secret radar. Like there must be some chief seagull sitting on top of a cliff somewhere, keeping watch with a very large telescope. And then he sends out a signal to all his friends: 'Food below, team—southwest from here. Dive! Dive! Dive!'"

Carly "Or they're just really good at smelling."

The girls giggle as they eat their sandwiches. The more crusts they throw at the seagulls, the more seagulls gather. Mai's mother tells them to stop. She says that as soon as their lunch has settled, they can go back into the water.

Mai "I think I'm ready for that contest. A surf-off between us."

Carly "Yeah, and your mum could be the judge."

Mai "So whoever loses has to wash the dishes tonight."

Carly "You're on!"

CHAPTER 4

The Surf-off

Soon the girls are back in the surf. They paddle out to the big waves. Mai's mother sits on her beach towel. She tells the girls she can get a better judge's view of them sitting down than standing up.

Mai (yelling) "Look, here comes a huge one."

Carly "It's a right-hander."

Mai "How do you know that?"

Carly "I saw it on a surf show on TV."

Mai "I'm gonna go for it."

Mai starts to paddle hard and manages to catch the wave. She gets a really good ride. Carly catches the next wave and washes straight over the top of Mai, who is trying to paddle back out.

Mai "You lose points for running into me."

Carly "No way! You lose points for getting in the way."

Carly and Mai keep catching waves, totally unaware that the waves have swept them outside the flagged area … until they hear a voice booming across the water: "Girls on the boogie boards—come into shore immediately and report to the lifeguard".

Mai "D'you think he's talking to us?"

Carly "Yeah, I think we might be outside the flags."

Mai "Look, Mum's waving a towel at us."

Carly and Mai paddle towards the shore. The lifeguard and Mai's mother are there to greet them, and neither of them looks very happy.

Carly "Uh-oh! I think we might be in trouble."

Mai "Well, it's not my fault."

Carly "But you're the one who said we should have a surf-off."

Mai "Yeah, but you agreed."

CHAPTER 5

Double Trouble

The lifeguard tells the girls that if they swim outside the flags, they could be in danger of getting caught in a rip. Mai's mother sends the girls back to the caravan for the rest of the afternoon.

Mai "What a drag! This is so dumb having to be inside on such a great day."

Carly "Yeah, how were we s'posed to know we were drifting outside the flags."

Mai "I guess we've just gotta be really careful and keep an eye on things next time."

Carly "Yeah, guess so."

Mai "So, who won the surf-off?"

Carly "I did ... and easily."

Mai "In your dreams."

Carly "We'll just have to ask your mum."

Later on, the girls ask Mai's mum who the winner is. She says that she's still deciding and she'll tell them after dinner. As they are clearing the table, both girls speak at the same time.

Carly and Mai "So who won?"

Mai's mum grins and tells the girls it was a draw. And their prize for both winning (and losing)? They both have to wash the dishes!

GIRLZ ROCK! Surfing Lingo

Mai   *Carly*

bombora An underwater reef which makes huge waves form way out to sea.

boogie board A small, light board for riding waves, which you usually lie on.

hang ten To ride a surfboard while standing on the edge of it with all 10 toes hanging over.

wetsuit A thick rubber suit that surfers wear to keep them warm in cold water.

wipe out When a surfer falls from their surfboard because they lose their balance.

GIRLZ ROCK!
Surfing Must-dos

⭐ Swim between the flags, or else!

⭐ Make sure that you use the right lingo when you are surfing, and talk like a surfer. Say things like "Cool man", "Hang ten" and "That wave really ripped".

⭐ The most important thing to remember to yell when you catch a good wave is "Girlz Rock!".

⭐ Never surf alone. If you have an accident and you're on your own, no-one is there to help you.

⭐ Always wear sunscreen with a Sun Protection Factor (SPF) of at least 15.

★ Wear board shorts so you look cool, but make sure they won't come off in a strong wave!

★ Have a leg rope on your board, which saves you swimming back into shore to get your board each time you fall off.

★ Make sure that if there's a rip in the surf, you stay well away from it.

GIRLZ ROCK!

Surfing Instant Info

- The longest surfboard ride ever recorded was 9.1 kilometres when a surfer caught a wave in the United Kingdom.

- World surfing championships for women started in 1979.

- When you surf down the face of a wave, then you surf back up the wave and you and your board fly into the air, you have just done an "airy".

- If you are surfing and you turn your board in a complete circle, you have done a "360".

Some surfers surf in sub-zero temperatures, such as in Ireland. To keep warm, they wear a wetsuit that covers every part of their body, even their head.

A right-hander is a wave that breaks to the right and a left-hander breaks to the left, as you face the beach.

The highest wave ever ridden struck in 1868 and was thought to be more than 15 metres high.

GIRLZ ROCK!
Think Tank

1 What does "SPF" stand for?

2 What is a left-hander?

3 Why do you need to surf between the flags at the beach?

4 When did world surfing championships start for women?

5 Would you rather meet a shark or a dolphin in the water?

6 How many fins does a twin fin surfboard have?

7 Why is the term "360" used in surfing?

8 What wipes out in a "wipe out"?

Answers

1. "SPF" stands for Sun Protection Factor.
2. A left-hander is a wave that breaks from right to left.
3. You need to surf between the flags so you don't get caught in a rip.
4. Women's world surfing championships started in 1979.
5. You'd probably rather meet a dolphin—it'll help you out if a shark comes along!
6. A twin fin surfboard has two fins—the name is a clue!
7. There are 360 degrees in a circle. You turn in a complete circle on the wave when you make a "360".
8. The surfer wipes out because they fall off their board.

How did you score?

- If you got 8 answers correct, then it's time to catch a wave, surf girl!

- If you got 6 answers correct, then you'll look cool in surf clothes but still might need an extra surf lesson or two.

- If you got fewer than 4 answers correct, then maybe having fun in a wave pool is more your thing.

Hey Girls!

I hope that you have as much fun reading my story as I have had writing it. I loved reading and writing stories when I was young.

At school, why don't you use "Surf Girls" as a play and you and your friends can be the actors.

Bring in a boogie board and beach towel from home to use as props. And you'll be able to wear your bathers if it's hot. You can pretend that you and your friends are about to go surfing at the beach.

So ... have you decided who is going to be Mai and who is going to be Carly?

Now, with your friends, read and act out this play in front of your classmates. It'll definitely make the whole class laugh.

You can also take the story home and get someone to act out the parts with you.

So, get ready to have more fun with your reading than Santa on Christmas Eve!

And remember, Girlz Rock!

GIRLZ ROCK!
When We Were Kids

Shey / *Jacqueline*

Shey talked to Jacqueline, another *Girlz Rock!* author

Shey "Did you ever see a shark in the surf when you were a kid?"

Jacqui "No, but I saw a big white whale when I was swimming once."

Shey "Really? Were you scared?"

Jacqui "No, but I was scared for the whale. I thought that someone might spear it or hurt it somehow."

Shey "So what did you do?"

Jacqui "I shooed it away."

Shey "What did you say?"

Jacqui "Dad, get out of the water!"

GIRLZROCK!
What a Laugh!

Q Who lives under the sea and paints pictures?

A Leonardo de Fishy.

GIRLZROCK!

Read about the fun that girls have in these GIRLZROCK! titles:

Hair Scare

Diary Disaster

Netball Showdown

The Sleepover

Bowling Buddies

School Play Stars

Pool Pals

Horsing Around

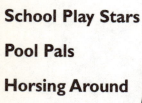

Girl Pirates

Surf Girls